STARTS HERE ...

NORTHERN TALES

First published in Great Britain in 2009 by
Young Writers, Remus House, Coltsfoot Drive,
Peterborough, PE2 9JX
Tel (01733) 890066 Fax (01733) 313524

SB ISBN 978-1-84431-929-9

Disclaimer
Young Writers has maintained every effort
to publish stories that will not cause offence.
Any stories, events or activities relating to individuals
should be read as fictional pieces and not construed
as real-life character portrayal.

FOREWORD

Since Young Writers was established in 1990, our aim has been to promote and encourage written creativity amongst children and young adults. By giving aspiring young authors the chance to be published, Young Writers effectively nurtures the creative talents of the next generation, allowing their confidence and writing ability to grow.

With our latest fun competition, *The Adventure Starts Here...* , primary school children nationwide were given the tricky challenge of writing a story with a beginning, middle and an end in just fifty words.

The diverse and imaginative range of entries made the selection process a difficult but enjoyable task with stories chosen on the basis of style, expression, flair and technical skill. A fascinating glimpse into the imaginations of the future, we hope you will agree that this entertaining collection is one that will amuse and inspire the whole family.

CONTENTS

THE MINI SAGAS

THE CLOWN

Suddenly as the clock struck twelve I saw my worst nightmare covered in blood, bruises and scars. As it came towards me slowly, I tried running but it caught me. I couldn't believe my eyes, it was a clown, it tried to kill me but sunrise came and it disappeared.

KAIDEN TURNER (10)
Christ Church Primary School, Manchester

THE TERRIFYING BEDROOM

I walked into my bedroom. I closed my silky
curtains and got into bed. I shut my eyes and
suddenly I heard my wardrobe slam shut.
I opened my eyes, terrified. I ran to my door
and tried to open it, but it would not open,
I was petrified.

CHLOE MITCHELL (10)
Christ Church Primary School, Manchester

THE SPOOKY CASTLE!

As I walked into the colossal castle, I made out a ghostly figure. I ran to the shattered window and tried to get out. My hand throbbed as I trapped it. Stalking me, the foreboding beast pulled me back and threw me into a room with rotting dead bodies. *Argh!*

MADISON VERITY-POWER (10)

Christ Church Primary School, Manchester

GOODBYE MY FRIEND

That day was a terribly sad day for Sophie. Hannah left to help the NSPCC in Africa. Sadness poured out of Sophie's heart, but she knew it was for good. Alisha, the girl Hannah was looking after sent postcards every week. Sophie very soon felt happiness in her sad heart.

GEORGIA MCKEVITT (10)
Christ Church Primary School, Manchester

THE MYSTERIOUS FIGURE

Cautiously, I entered the derelict house. Everything was dead. Also the wind was a wolf howling. I shivered. Suddenly, I saw a pale white face ... Petrified I followed it and its eyes glared at me. I screamed and sprinted, but it was still waiting for me. What should I do?

ELEANOR DRURY (10)
Christ Church Primary School, Manchester

THE ORPHAN

There once was a girl from England and her name
was Gabby and she wanted a child. She found a
child from Poland; she was called Katy, who was
lost and alone. She was cold and starving,
so Gabby got her some food and gave her
a big, big cuddle.

JAMES MOSEY (10)
Christ Church Primary School, Manchester

HORRENDOUS HAUNTED HOUSE

Bang! As the door shut Dad ran to the colossal car. Barry was in his house on his own. Suddenly I saw a transparent figure. It suddenly faded away, pillows and books started to fly all over the room. I was petrified. I didn't know what to do!

LEONI HARRISON (10)
Christ Church Primary School, Manchester

IT ISN'T FAIR ON THAT GIRL

Kidda was at home with her aggressive mum. She came down the stairs and there was her mum ready to charge. So she quietly crept behind her and ran away. Soon she bumped into Dad and started weeping on him. Both of them went to his flat forever ... maybe.

CHLOE CROXON (10)
Christ Church Primary School, Manchester

THE LITTLE GIRL WHO ENDED UP WITH A FANTASTIC FAMILY

As I walked through the bushes I saw a pale face and I didn't know what to do. I was so scared but I walked a little closer and this woman called Agnes hugged me in her arms and stroked me on the back and gave me a kiss.

KAI BLACK (10)

Christ Church Primary School, Manchester

DEAR DIARY, I'M BEING BULLIED IN SCHOOL

Dear, diary, during yesterday I was nearby the hall, but suddenly a gang came up to me and they're called Mike, Sam, Will, Chris and Jazz. They kicked me in the belly. I felt sick. I really hate them. I wish they would just leave me alone …

JESSICA GRUNDY (10)
Christ Church Primary School, Manchester

THE TORTURED HOUSE

One wistful night while I was camping it started to pour down. We all needed to have a shelter, so we went to the nearest house. Then while we were sleeping in sleeping bags I heard a noise. Then I saw a mysterious figure in the hallway.
Oh no ...

TEEYA MEMORY (10)
Christ Church Primary School, Manchester

THE GHOSTLY DREAM

The boy had a scary dream about a ghost chasing him slowly. Then he woke up screaming and the pillows started jiggling. The bed started wobbling and the boy got scared. His mum came in and helped him from being sad. Then the little boy got cheered up.

NATHAN STEWART (10)
Christ Church Primary School, Manchester

THE HAUNTED ROOM

I walked to the room and picked up the pillow. The pillow jumped off the table. I went on the computer and it wouldn't turn on. It was very peculiar. Something flew past me and through the brick wall, was it a ghost? What could this disgusting figure be ... ?

ADAM STEVENSON (9)
Christ Church Primary School, Manchester

THE TREASURE BE MINE

Suddenly, the black kraken ship came sailing as
fast as the wind, crushing every wave as it went
past! Finally we got there and began the fierce
battle of two brave captains. After two long
disturbing hours we began to feel the blades in
our flesh. Then victory, I won!

ANNABEL DOWD (10)
Christ Church Primary School, Manchester

THE GHOSTLY SPIRIT

Once upon a time there was a spirit that was in my room for a long, long time. After a while I ran to the jar. Then I picked it up and my hand slipped and I dropped it and a ghost came out and then he disappeared ...

CHARLOTTE ODELL (9)
Christ Church Primary School, Manchester

THE MOST DANGEROUS SECRET IN THE WORLD

Josh must find out the most dangerous secret ever in the deep forest of the Mexican jungle with a deadly international hit man on his trail. He must find the secret in the temple of doom, in a plastic bottle, it lies. He reaches out ... he pulls it ... *kerching!*

CONNOR HURST (10)
Leeside Community Primary School, Heckmondwike

FROG, GIRAFFE AND HIPPO

One day there was a frog and he spoke to the giraffe but the giraffe couldn't hear him. So he found a hippopotamus, the frog stood on the hippo's back. 'Hi,' said the frog, but the giraffe still couldn't hear him. Frog was silent.
Nice snack, thought Hippo.

CASEY BRIDGES (10)
Leeside Community Primary School, Heckmondwike

GETTING FIRED

It was time … the boss wanted me, not sure why,
but he did. I'm so scared.
'What's your name?' the boss asked.
'Erm, Homer, Sir.' I replied.
'To put this delicately - you're *fired!'* shouted Mr
Burns. 'Release the hounds!'
'Argh, Doh! That's how I lost my job,' sighed
Homer Simpson.

MARK DAVIES (10)
Leeside Community Primary School, Heckmondwike

THE UNEXPECTED DISASTER

It was dark and gloomy at the scientists' HQ.
They were mixing potions way into the night,
then suddenly *boom!* the whole building exploded,
argh! Scientists ran out in all different directions,
kicking and screaming like little girls, lights
flickered everywhere, the whole town
was awake. *Thud, oops!*

EMMA LEES (10)
Leeside Community Primary School, Heckmondwike

DEEP UNDER THE SEA

Deep under the sea nobody knows what lies
beneath the seaweed; a reef shark hunting for its
tea, the poor little fishies were hunting for their
tea. As the shark approached the fish ...
he stopped for a cup of tea.

KENNEDY CLAUGHTON (10)

Leeside Community Primary School, Heckmondwike

JAMIE AND KEENOP

There once was a boy who lived in America. He loved adventures and he saw a UFO. It looked so bright. An alien came out of nowhere and said, 'Ig lo,' then he knew that he said 'I come in peace' and they played together and they became BOFs.

MARIYA HUSMAN (10)
Leeside Community Primary School, Heckmondwike

A TRIP TO MEXICO

Arriving in Mexico was a dream come true when I saw the Golden Isle. When we docked the isle was grey and infested with crabs and litter, not to mention a squid! I was so glad my sister had a sea creature scare gun! *Bang!* and the animals had gone.

ASHLEY TASKER (9)
Leeside Community Primary School, Heckmondwike

THE DRIFT

One Monday at go-karting, Tom and I paid. We set off out of the pits! Tom went first but he had spun on the first corner. I drifted around him, crossing the line as the champion!

SAM MALTAS (10)

Leeside Community Primary School, Heckmondwike

HOLIDAY

I went on holiday to France. I could not speak French. I was walking down the street and someone just came up to me and started to talk to me … in English!

SOPHIE HIGGINS (10)

Leeside Community Primary School, Heckmondwike

PARTY ANIMAL

Gorilla wasn't kind to any animals in the wild.
He went to his door and found an envelope in
the letter box. Opening it, an invitation to
a party fell out!
He got there and started to have fun! and he said,
'I'm actually happy,' and did a break dance!

LUCY NELSON (9)
Leeside Community Primary School, Heckmondwike

THE MAGIC TREE

The magic tree was a mysterious tree with a wand carved into the trunk. When his roots snapped Rabbit knew only Sun and his brother Rain could help. Sun shone on the wand and the rain wet the wand and the tree lit up like a light bulb and flowered.

EMMA PITCHFORTH (10)
Leeside Community Primary School, Heckmondwike

TENT NAPPER

One dark and gloomy night the tent napper was out and about. He stole someone's tent when they were sleeping in it. He stole someone's tent when they were brushing their teeth. He stole someone's tent when they were singing. What a horrible, crazy, ugly and sneaky tent napper.

CALLA ROBINSON-SOUTHON (10)

Leeside Community Primary School, Heckmondwike

UNTITLED

One day a little boy set off to see his grandma.
His friend came with him. They also had a little
game of football! Then he and his friend saw
Linda, so Linda started to walk with them to
Grandma's, but when they turned up
she was not in!

KELSEY FIRTH (10)
Leeside Community Primary School, Heckmondwike

POP STAR

Elizabeth stepped onto the dance mat ...
Suddenly lights blazed into her eyes, she heard
music and the crowd cheering. She looked
around. Stood on the stage, everybody watching
her, she wondered what to do ...
'Sing,' said Sarah, 'Welcome to Girls Aloud!'

DANA JEFFERSON (10)
Leeside Community Primary School, Heckmondwike

POKÉMON WORLD

One dark day in the valley land of Arsias, a
terrible mistake had happened. Darkrye had
escaped jail so Arsias went to hunt him down.
When he found Darkrye he used stun spores.
He took him back and locked him up.
Darkrye was trapped and will never escape ...

KYLE BARKER (10)

Leeside Community Primary School, Heckmondwike

RISK OF DEATH

One stormy night at the army base there was a sergeant called Mark. He was strange because every time you looked at him he wandered off. So one of the soldiers followed him then discovered that he was planning to destroy the Earth. He started it, then a big bang …

DENALEA BRAND ROBINSON (10)
Leeside Community Primary School, Heckmondwike

HAUNTED MANSION

A girl, all alone, sat on a creaky chair. She heard
a noise. She shouted, 'Who's there?' She was
scared … 'Help!' she screamed. The black
monster crept out of the darkness …
Too bad it's a movie.

LORNA WHITLEY

Leeside Community Primary School, Heckmondwike

UNTITLED

After going on the big dipper, I bought some candyfloss. Dark clouds appeared, lightning struck, my snack was frazzled! It turned into a monster. We went on the ghost train. He fell in love with Medusa. He lived on the ghost train with Medusa ... until somebody ate him.

INDIA HUTCHASON (11)
Low Furness CE Primary School, Great Urswick

FAIRGROUND

'Mum, Mum, where are you?'
'I'm on a ride.'
'Please, please come Mum. I'm really scared.
Can you hear me?'
'I'm over here son, but I'm dying. There was
a man with a gun. He shot me.'
'Mum, can you hear me? Mum, please, *noo*,
wake up Mum, wake up.'

CONNOR KELLY (11)
Low Furness CE Primary School, Great Urswick

THE LOCH NESS MONSTER

Max went to Scotland with his mum. When they got there they went to the loch and Max saw the Loch Ness monster. He ran back to the hotel and told his mum. She went to the loch - it was a big stick!

DOMINIC BOWLER (11)

Low Furness CE Primary School, Great Urswick

WHAT A DISASTER

A loud smash of glass down in the kitchen, dogs
running up the stairs, torches on the landing,
a creak of my bedroom door. Two men stood
in my bedroom doorway. The rescue team,
they're talking about a hurricane called
Hishma in Ulverston.

SAM BALDWIN (11)

Low Furness CE Primary School, Great Urswick

THE END OF THE UNIVERSE IS NIGH!

There was a whizzing sound, Kelvin ran away but a thin blue beam hit him, he screamed as he fell to the ground. Mark was watching from around the corner, terrified, he saw seven dome-shaped robots land and fire more beams at the trees. Then the park went *boom!*

BEN COOPER (10)
Low Furness CE Primary School, Great Urswick

THE BIG BOOM!

The mad scientist went mad pouring in different potions. *Pop, pop, pop,* bubbles came out. A dog jumped into the room smashing the glasses. 'Stop, stop, stop, la, la, la, la, mad, mad, mad,' shouted the scientist.
A tiny drop of another liquid made the world blow up. *Boom!*

LUKE BASKERVILLE (10)
Low Furness CE Primary School, Great Urswick

THE HORSE ACCIDENT

Cantering down the racetrack. Demi screamed,
Laura reared at the jump. Demi tumbled over
Laura's neck. *New-naw* came the ambulance.
Demi was at hospital, her elbow had broken, she
was in theatre when they put wires in her elbow.
How brave she was, coming home
and riding again ...

YASMIN BUTLER (10)
Low Furness CE Primary School, Great Urswick

SIMON'S ROOM

Simon walked in the door from school and ran upstairs and saw in horror a tidy room. Simon's mum came in the back door and sat in the lounge. So Simon came thumping downstairs and burst into the room and said, 'Thanks for tidying my room, it needed that.'

ROWAN HEATON (10)
Low Furness CE Primary School, Great Urswick

UNTITLED

There were three girls having a sleepover when suddenly they saw a flashing light outside the window. They looked outside the window and they saw a spaceship. The aliens were wrecking the garden. They went to tell their mum and when they got there the aliens were gone for good.

EVE PROCTER (9)
Low Furness CE Primary School, Great Urswick

THE LAST MINUTE

With a minute to go, Gerrard fouled Ronaldo
in the penalty area. Ronaldo equalised and the
fans looked on in despair! Gerrard, horrified and
determined shouted, 'Come on England,
keep it together!'
Kick-off. Rooney to Lampard brings it forward
past Deco. Through ball to Gerrard,
one touch, *gooaaalll!*

BEN GILMOUR (10)
St Catherine's School, Didsbury

THE FRIGHTENING REFLECTION

She looked into the mirror. She saw an indescribable creature. It was coming closer, blood dripping down its face. Its arm came out and grabbed her. She screamed. It started to pull her into the mirror. The girl struggled but the creature was strong. She eventually got sucked in.

KATHLEEN O'CONNOR (10)
St Catherine's School, Didsbury

IN TROUBLE

I paced the floor, my hands sweating, my heart
pounding like a drum. What if she screamed in
my face? I hadn't done wrong. Oh? Maybe a little.
My knees were knocking madly. The doorknob
twisted. And a dark figure entered the room.
The head teacher was there ...

MADELEINE HEALEY (10)
St Catherine's School, Didsbury

ESCAPE FROM PRISON

I was crouched down in the dark shadows,
sweating, trying not to make any noise. I crept
along the corridor hoping no one would find me.
I got to the gate. Freedom was in sight.
As I started to run a firm hand grasped
my shoulder …

GEORGIE CONLAN (10)

St Catherine's School, Didsbury

CLIMBING THE WALL OF DEATH

As I climbed up it, I realised that I was 20 feet off
the ground. So I decided to climb down because
I was really scared. Then when I got down
I was called a baby by my cousin because
I couldn't climb the climbing frame.

AHMAD KASSIR (10)
St Catherine's School, Didsbury

TRAPPED

'Help!' You hear him cry, he can never get out. It all started when he was digging holes in the beach, but he dug a really deep hole and then jumped in. He always tries to get out but the sand pours in when he tries to climb up it.

THOMAS BENNETT (10)
St Catherine's School, Didsbury

THE FOREST FIGURE

The hulking dark figure sniffed the air. I moved
back into light. I looked up seeing a gap between
the thick leaves. The figure crept forward.
I fell back banging my head on a tree trunk.
The figure stuck his giant grey hand into the light.
Could it be ... ?

JAMES D'SOUZA (10)
St Catherine's School, Didsbury

I'M IN TROUBLE

Waiting, waiting and waiting my heart pounding
like a drum. The head teacher's handle twisted.
Tears dripping down my cheeks, wondering what
would happen next. What did I do? Well apart
from putting chewing gum in Joe's hair
I've been very good, my hands sweating,
shall I run for it? ...

MACAULEY MORAN (9)
St Catherine's School, Didsbury

SPACE

Youngest boy in space ... I was with my mate
Caine. *Look at the stars*, I thought. We were going
down the big fall now! All of a sudden
it stopped ...
'I won't be going on the indoor roller coaster,
Space again!' I said to Caine.

THOMAS ELLISON (10)
St Catherine's School, Didsbury

THE DISCOVERY

His torch shone upon the seal to the coffin of King Asru. Professor Clarke knew then his long search was over. He smiled to himself, he'd beaten the mummy's curse. He carefully opened the heavy lid and as he gazed at the mummy a blood-curdling scream was heard ...

LYDIA CHARLES (10)

St Catherine's School, Didsbury

THAT SINKING FEELING

The sky was like a dark blanket above me.
I could hardly feel my feet in the icy water. In the
distance I could hear faint cries. Will I ever see
America or my family again? I watched the Titanic
disappear before my very eyes.
Suddenly I woke up ...

VICTORIA SMYTH (10)
St Catherine's School, Didsbury

UNTITLED

I woke up, I was cold, sweating and scared.
I didn't know where I was. It was raining, I felt like crying. 'Help me!' I cried, my heart was beating really fast. I heard someone banging against something. I dropped to my knees and cried, something was moving near me …

LAURELLE DALE (10)
St Catherine's School, Didsbury

I DID IT

'Max!' called Mum. 'We need to talk.'
I froze, she knew about the broken window.
Wiping my sweating forehead I dragged myself
downstairs, ran into the kitchen, threw myself
on the floor screeching, 'I did it!
'Oh,' she replied. 'I just wondered if you
fancied the cinema tonight, perhaps not!'

MAX GODDARD (10)
St Catherine's School, Didsbury

TICKLY TOES!

One night in bed, I could feel something touching
the tip of my toes. It felt tickly, soft and strange.
I was scared and frightened and couldn't get to
sleep. So, I nervously looked under the red, soft,
fluffy quilt and opening my eyes wider
I saw cute Cuddles Bear.

FIONA TAYLOR (9)
St Catherine's School, Didsbury

DANGER MOUNTAIN

I was on my hike. I saw a very big mountain called
Danger Mountain. We had heard stories about it
but we didn't believe them, so we climbed up.
At the top there was a cave, so we went inside,
the only light was from two big glowing eyes.
Help!

CHRISTOPHER FOLLOWS (9)

St Catherine's School, Didsbury

THE MONSTER DOG

I was running, running from the monster. I tripped
onto the hard ground, the monster licked my
face. It pushed me down with sharp claws.
Its head lowered, I felt its hot breath, I thought
it was going to eat me!
I woke up seeing it was, Benjy, my dog.

NATHAN DONEGAN (10)
St Catherine's School, Didsbury

AFRAID

It was midnight and the grandfather clock on the
landing struck 12. Suddenly, I felt an icy chill as the
floorboards creaked outside my bedroom.
I reluctantly got out of my bed, opened the door,
where a pair of green glowing eyes appeared,
followed by a loud miaow. 'Hello Tiddles.'

REBECCA BERRINGTON (9)
St Catherine's School, Didsbury

FIRE FOREST

Gilbert the one-legged schoolboy sat on the
patio looking at the forest, which backed onto his
house. Suddenly he shouted loudly,
'The forest is on fire!'
Quickly his parents ran outside but when they
realised what was happening, they laughed, it was
only the jumbled, shiny, red autumn leaves.

JUSTINE KEELING (10)
St Catherine's School, Didsbury

CREEPY SOUNDS

It was in the middle of the night when
I was awoken by a strange sound, *creak, creak.*
I slowly opened one eye, then I heard it again,
louder, *creak.* I opened my other eye.
Click, went the light switch.
'It's only me luv, just putting all your
clothes away.'

JACK SHAW (9)
St Catherine's School, Didsbury

SUDDENLY

Suddenly an SOS message came over the radio.
The voice of a captain calling for help. 'Off
Queensland, Voyager, urgent sea and air rescue,
ship sinking, 500 passengers; men,
women and children.'
Brave and courageous RAF and coastguards set
out on their mission through stormy weather
to save many lives.

DARRAGH O'LEARY

St Catherine's School, Didsbury

OH SUGAR

I was in bed that Christmas Eve but I couldn't
sleep because I was worried that Santa would
forget our house this year. Suddenly I heard
something from downstairs. Armed only with
a torch I crept down there and *whack!*
'Oh sugar, I've knocked out Santa!'

RACHAEL KEELING (10)

St Catherine's School, Didsbury

THE BASEMENT

When Molly asked if we could play a game,
I wasn't too sure. I don't like the basement.
'You first,' I said.
Moments later my mobile rang - Molly. I switched
it off and smiled. I never did like Molly.
No one goes in the basement anymore.
People think it's haunted.

ELLA POWER (10)
St Catherine's School, Didsbury

UNTITLED

One day I went to McDonald's and I got a kid's meal and I got a toy with it, then we went home. It was quiet and then we went inside and no one was there. We couldn't hear a thing. We thought everyone had gone shopping, then *'Boo!'*

KIERAN WRIGHT O'CONNELL (9)
St Catherine's School, Didsbury

MYSTERY 'TAIL'

I was running, down the street. It was getting closer, closer, closer. *Ahh!* I woke up on the floor at the side of my bed. There was a shadow coming towards me, something was under my bed. There was heavy breathing. Something was tickling my feet. *Woof!*

'Oh! Hello Milo!'

REBECCA CULLINANE (10)

St Catherine's School, Didsbury

THE WHITBY SPOOK (HAUNTED HOUSE)

My mum remembers the house being dark, dusty and deserted. She and friends slowly walked through the narrow corridors, hearts racing, stomachs churning, when suddenly a tall, spooky figure appeared. They screamed and ran with the figure chasing them. They saw an exit and hastily escaped with relief and laughter.

ROISIN MARIE TOWEY (10)
St Catherine's School, Didsbury

THE LEGENDARY ANSWER

There it was. The mysterious legend that had puzzled mankind for centuries. My shirt was torn and my arm was bleeding badly. And then …

'Niamh!'

'What? Oh, is it the holy grail?' Then I looked at the board, it said thirty times ten equals …

'Sorry, Sir. I dozed off again!'

NIAMH SHARKEY MILUM (10)

St Catherine's School, Didsbury

DESERTED!

The house was dark, I couldn't hear a sound. All of a sudden I felt deserted, alone and frightened. Then I heard a stomp, stomp, stomping noise behind the wooden door. So I opened it to see who it was, or what it was.
'Oh hello Sam, what a surprise!'

CAITLYN JOHNSON (10)
St Catherine's School, Didsbury

THE CREEPY JUNGLE

As we slashed and hacked at the thick jungle
bushes we realised that this would be a longer
journey than we thought it would. Looking at the
jungle floor, it moved as if it was alive.
I had a feeling that it wasn't the only thing alive
and watching me.

JORDAN HAGGERTY (10)

St Catherine's School, Didsbury

PANTING FOR BREATH

I was panting for breath. As I reached the surface
I started to panic. Water rushed all around me.
I went under again and then I laughed and realised
it was just a paddling pool.

HANNAH METCALFE (8)
St Joseph's RC Primary School, Sunderland

UNDER THE SEA

Under the sea there lived a human who was the king. The king's name was Waterman. There was a prince who was the son of the king.
One day the king's son planned to kill his father, but the plan didn't work because the soldiers told the king ...

JITHIN TOJI (8)
St Joseph's RC Primary School, Sunderland

THE MYSTERIOUS THING IN THE WARDROBE

Lucy wakes up at midnight. She realises it's
quiet around her, the only sound she can hear is
the thumping of her heart. Suddenly she spots
something green glowing in her wardrobe.
Lucy is scared but she wants to know what it is.
Then she sees it, it's a ghost.

ACHSAH FINNEY (8)
St Joseph's RC Primary School, Sunderland

PERFECT HENRY

Henry went to Peter's room with a freezing ice cream and threw it at Peter. He wanted to do it again after lunch. His mum told him not to, so he did as he was told all the time,. Now his name is 'Perfect Henry', Peter is just called Peter.

DANIEL BROWN (9)

St Joseph's RC Primary School, Sunderland

ALONG THE PIER

As Katie dawdled slowly across the pier the waves crashed against the sides. Katie carried on walking forward through the pitch-black mist. She had been told to come here but by whom? Katie couldn't see anyone. Then suddenly, through the fog, a black figure stood impatiently …

TONI BEVAN (8)
St Joseph's RC Primary School, Sunderland

ON THE SEA

For some reason the water was hot, then a big
splash was heard. All of the fish had gone, then
'Lilly it's time to come out of the bath now.'
No wonder it was hot water.

CHLOE MACKEL (8)
St Joseph's RC Primary School, Sunderland

SHADOWS

Kate came to the forest because they were going
to celebrate Kate's birthday there. Then came
shadows everywhere. What was she going to do?
Then balloons popped out - it was
only her family.

JANNIE PINEDA (8)
St Joseph's RC Primary School, Sunderland

DOOR TROUBLE

Liam put the key into the lock but it would not fit.
He started to panic then he looked at the door,
the number was two. This was not his house.
He walked away laughing.

ELEANOR DUNCAN (8)
St Joseph's RC Primary School, Sunderland

WHO IS IT?

'Hello? Anybody home?' My voice echoed through the air. My legs were shivering, you could even hear the air I was breathing.
'Yes I am home. Oh, sorry are you cold? I'll get something so you can huddle up,' said a voice.
Then he never came back again.

ARSHA MATHEW (11)
St Joseph's RC Primary School, Sunderland

THE SKELETON KEY

Kelly looked at her present surprised. It was a key. She stared at it and said, 'It's a silver skeleton key!' Suddenly a wooden door appeared and sucked her in. '30 seconds until self-destruction.' She tried to bash down the door. She desperately tried, but it was too late! ...

LAUREN BROWN (10)

St Joseph's RC Primary School, Sunderland

THE TERRIFYING JUMP

My legs were shaking. I thought I was going to fall. I wanted to get down but I was a wimp. All of my friends were staring. *'Go!'* shouted my worst enemy and the immature school bully. I jumped ... Then I heard a big clap. I dived into the pool.

CHARLOTTE POTTS (11)
St Joseph's RC Primary School, Sunderland

WRONG DECISIONS!

Lizzy was walking on the sandy beach watching all
the children play in the sea. She had to be home
by 7.00pm. It was 6.55pm already.
Lizzy jumped into the sea.
Three days later the forensics were searching.
In the freezing cold sea was a pale dead body.

BETH KENNEDY (11)
St Joseph's RC Primary School, Sunderland

THE STRANGER

Suddenly the door creaked and swung open,
I could hear footsteps stamping down the stairs.
It was getting closer and closer. I started to
scream. I started to run but the wind lashed
the door closed.
It was dark and I was all alone. It was damp.
A man appeared!

DOMINIQUE SCOTT (10)
St Joseph's RC Primary School, Sunderland

THE HAUNTED CASTLE

I froze still in that spot in the castle. I could hear voices calling my name. I looked around, I could hear footsteps coming closer to me. I looked around then I saw it. It had red eyes, a green, slimy body with yellow puss coming out of it.

EMMA MARGETSON (10)
St Joseph's RC Primary School, Sunderland

LIGHTS OUT

It was dark in all of New York. Max was crossing the road determined to get to his apartment before midnight as it was New Year. He could hear nothing coming, he could not see anything either, so he crossed the road. But then in a small simple second. *Crash!*

JACK HENDERSON (11)

St Joseph's RC Primary School, Sunderland

DOWN AND UNDER

My hands sweated and I shook like I was in the Arctic. I opened the door to the dark room. Suddenly I fell, *'Argh.'* I got up and looked around. The only light was a small lamp. I lurked on further but there was nobody there. Where was I?

JOSEPH CLIFF (11)
St Joseph's RC Primary School, Sunderland

SHIPWRECK

Matt And Matilda were at their aunt's house with their cousin Gregory. She owned a shipwreck. They went to have a look around. Matt spotted a case and called everyone over. It was locked! They smashed it open ... to find it was full of *gold!*

JACK ROBINSON (10)

St Joseph's RC Primary School, Sunderland

THE TERRIBLE MONSTER!

One day I saw a big monster in the river so I ran home and told everyone about it. I found someone who had seen what happened then he tried to get a man to kill it. They worked as a team, the monster was screaming ...

SARAH RIDDELL (10)

St Joseph's RC Primary School, Sunderland

HORROR IN THE NIGHT

On Monday night I heard a knock. I ran
downstairs. I shivered, but it was only the clock.
I tiptoed up the stairs. I heard a creak. Suddenly
I felt so weak. I shook to the toilet,
I heard a scream from Mum.
I woke up, it was a dream.

BRAD WALLACE (10)
St Joseph's RC Primary School, Sunderland

CINDERELLA

One day Cinderella got a letter in the door. She could not get it because her ugly stepsisters got it first. They opened it and read it out. It was for Cinderella. They read it out to her and they would not give it to her. She was sad.

NEVE GARDENER (10)

St Joseph's RC Primary School, Sunderland

TRAIN TRACK!

I was on a walk in the dead of night when suddenly … a train track appeared. I decided to explore. I was walking up the train track when I heard *choo choo!* It was a train. *'Argh!'* I ran quickly. In came my mam, it was only a bad dream.

EMMA FORD (10)

St Joseph's RC Primary School, Sunderland

THE LOST IDOL!

It was there right in front of me, all gold, worth
£1 billion. I lunged out to grab the idol. Suddenly
it turned to dust, the room shook, the booby
traps started. I had to get out.
There was a loud yell, it was my brother
waking me up!

CLAUDIA SPOOR (9)
St Joseph's RC Primary School, Sunderland

MAN WITH THE SAW

One night the moon was full, I walked down the
street when a man jumped out with a chainsaw,
then my life flashed before my eyes and then he
yelled, 'Stop, I am just cutting the trees in
my garden, sorry if I scared you.'
'It's OK,' I said.

JOSEPH BOWEY (9)

St Joseph's RC Primary School, Sunderland

THE DARKNESS

I was walking down the road, it was very dark, then I paused. It felt like something was behind me ... Suddenly I turned around but there was nothing there, then a hand grabbed my shoulder, it pulled me back and I was into the darkness!

LIAM SCULLION (10)

St Joseph's RC Primary School, Sunderland

CHEEKY MONKEY

Cheeky Monkey lived in the forest with his family.
He had no friends because he was nasty to them.
After a while Cheeky Monkey was trying to be
nice by saying sorry to the animals and giving
them gifts. Everyone started to be his friend and
they all partied.

SOPHIE BURNETT (10)
St Joseph's RC Primary School, Sunderland

A BIZARRE EXPERIMENT

Paul decided to go to his lab and mix liquids
to create sodium bicarbonate to explode his
mother's clean home. A major catastrophe
erupted before you could blink, *boom, bang,*
right in his dirty face.
Paul's mother's house lived to tell the tale of
her son's dirty face.

JEMINE PEMU (9)

St Joseph's RC Primary School, Sunderland

A JOURNEY BACK HOME

I was sitting when suddenly the car's back
seat shook, then I froze in fear when I heard a
scratching noise. I took a deep breath and looked
what it was. Suddenly I stopped shaking
because it was only a baby chimpanzee.
When we got home, I looked after it.

HERSHEY LOZADA (9)
St Joseph's RC Primary School, Sunderland

A JOURNEY BACK HOME

I was sitting when suddenly the train shook, then I heard a scratching and squeaking noise. I took a deep breath and then I looked up and saw that it was a mouse making the noise, when suddenly I realised that it was only a dream.

EMMA DAVIES (10)
St Joseph's RC Primary School, Sunderland

TOO FAR AWAY

I was sitting and shaking like milk bottles on a milk
cart and suddenly we stopped. I felt a lump in my
throat and I realised that I was in a rocket
ship to Pluto.

EVE HAWES (10)
St Joseph's RC Primary School, Sunderland

SNOW WHITE

Snow White was a girl who lived with seven dwarves. A witch got mad because Snow White was the prettiest girl in the world. She wanted to kill Snow White so she gave Snow White a poisoned apple. Snow White ate the apple and died.

HOLLY HENDERSON

St Joseph's RC Primary School, Sunderland

THE HAUNTED HOUSE

It was a stormy night. Lisa was walking through the graveyard and found a house for shelter. She went inside. Suddenly the door slammed shut. She tried to open it but it wouldn't open. She explored the house. She saw cobwebs, spiders and bats. Suddenly she heard a loud scream …

RIYA RAJU

St Joseph's RC Primary School, Sunderland

UNTITLED

I was screaming in pain when he touched my skin. What had he done to me? All I can remember was walking home after having a drink with my friends and then a man hit me with a cricket bat.

MATTHEW FLETCHER

St Joseph's RC Primary School, Sunderland

UNTITLED

Cinderella got a letter from the prince. He was asking if she could go to the ball. She wasn't allowed. Cinderella's godmother gave her a dress. Cinderella went off to the ball. She danced all night but when the clock struck 12 she had to leave.

MADELLA JUNIA
St Joseph's RC Primary School, Sunderland

UNTITLED

It was a stormy night. Rose was sitting in her
bedroom when a magical door opened.
She was scared. Rose went in. Rose was amazed.
There were flowers that could talk.
Suddenly there was a scream. When she looked it
wasn't a small or a big thing, it was huge!

ANUMOL JOHNSON
St Joseph's RC Primary School, Sunderland

UNTITLED

The computer began to beep. The building
began to shake. I dove for cover. What are they
trying to tell us? Everyone was nervous, can it be
explained? Is there such a thing as an alien?
I was so scared and worried I trembled with fear.

CHLOÉ FAIRWEATHER
St Joseph's RC Primary School, Sunderland

UNTITLED

It was a long day. Clare's dress was sweaty, her socks smelled. She opened the door and saw a cake on the table along with all her favourite food. Her eyes popped out. She wanted to taste some. She was about to try. The cake was hard.
'April Fool!'
'Mum?'

RESHMA GEORGE
St Joseph's RC Primary School, Sunderland

UNTITLED

Long ago a farmer lived with his wife and two children, happily. They had lots of crops so they never grew hungry. They had an easy life. All was going well until one day when they saw that one of the sheep had a baby. They were really happy.

JESLIN MATHEW
St Joseph's RC Primary School, Sunderland

UNTITLED

The panda went to the arena to find out who became Dragon Warrior. The panda tied some fireworks to his bum and lit them. The fireworks went out, but suddenly he took off. He landed in front of the Dragon Warrior and Panda's dream came true.

HARRY JEWITT

St Joseph's RC Primary School, Sunderland

UNTITLED

My legs trembled as I stepped inside. The wind
rushed through my ears. My heart was pounding.
Whatever was going on it sent shivers down my
spine, I wanted to go back home but my friends
were out there thinking I was a coward.

ANN ANDREAS
St Joseph's RC Primary School, Sunderland

UNTITLED

Snow White opened the door. Standing there was an old lady holding a basket of apples. The old lady offered Snow White an apple. Snow White said, 'Yes.' The old lady gave Snow White the brightest apple, Snow White bit into the apple and fell flat on the ground, poisoned.

REBECCA DIXON
St Joseph's RC Primary School, Sunderland

UNTITLED

Cinderella was cleaning when a letter came through the door from the prince. She opened it and it was an invitation to the prince's ball. Cinderella put it in her room but when she went to clean the bedrooms, she saw the ugly sisters trying on their beautiful dresses.

GEORGY CATCHESIDE

St Joseph's RC Primary School, Sunderland

THE ADVENTURE STARTS HERE ... NORTHERN TALES

INFORMATION

We hope you have enjoyed reading this book - and that you will continue to enjoy it in the coming years.

If you like reading and writing, drop us a line or give us a call and we'll send you a free information pack. Alternatively visit our website at www.youngwriters.co.uk

Write to:
Young Writers Information,
Remus House,
Coltsfoot Drive,
Peterborough,
PE2 9JX

Tel: (01733) 890066
Email: youngwriters@forwardpress.co.uk